Permission to reproduce the following is gratefully acknowledged:

"Tannen Honig (Pine Honey)" © 2019 by Eric Carle; "Cheese" © 2019 by Benji Davies; "Cake" © 2019 by Isabelle Arsenault;
"Ramen" © 2019 by Dan Santat; "Salad!" © 2019 by Greg Pizzoli; "Strawberry Daifuku" © 2019 by Misa Saburi;
"Berries" © 2019 by Brigette Barrager; "French Fries" © 2019 by Laurie Keller; "Paella" © 2019 by Felicita Sala;
"Chicken Alfredo" © 2019 by Shannon Wright; "Pizza" © 2019 by Matthew Cordell; "Pitaya Fruit" © 2019 by Juliet Menéndez;
"Matzo Ball Soup" © 2019 by Karen Katz; "Ice Cream" © 2019 by Aki.

Henry Holt and Company, *Publishers since 1866*
Henry Holt® is a registered trademark of Macmillan Publishing Group, LLC
120 Broadway, New York, NY 10271 • mackids.com

Compilation copyright © 2019 by Eric Carle

ISBN 978-1-250-29514-9
Library of Congress Control Number 2018955721

Our books may be purchased in bulk for promotional, educational, or business use. Please contact your local bookseller or the Macmillan
Corporate and Premium Sales Department at (800) 221-7945 ext. 5442 or by email at MacmillanSpecialMarkets@macmillan.com.

First edition, 2019
Printed in China by RR Donnelley Asia Printing Solutions Ltd., Dongguan City, Guangdong Province

1 3 5 7 9 10 8 6 4 2

Eric Carle and Friends

What's Your Favorite Food?

Aki • Isabelle Arsenault • Brigette Barrager • Matthew Cordell

Benji Davies • Karen Katz • Laurie Keller • Juliet Menéndez

Greg Pizzoli • Misa Saburi • Felicita Sala

Dan Santat • Shannon Wright

GODWINBOOKS

Henry Holt and Company

NEW YORK

TANNEN HONIG
(PINE HONEY)
Eric Carle

Many years ago, when I grew up as a small boy in Germany, I loved honey (*honig* in German). Honig on farmers' bread, with some butter spread on first, is perfect. Later, when I had grown up, I discovered tannen honig. (*Tannen* are pine trees.) This honey is the best honey in the world, in my opinion. That is, rich and dark like the pine forest itself. The first step in making tannen honig is for insects to drill little holes into the needles of pine trees for the sweet juice. Then bees cleverly and shamelessly steal that juice from the

insects by tickling them so that the poor aphids release the concentrated juice—jumping up and down and laughing, I suspect. The bees, now loaded with that juice, return to the hive, where worker bees manufacture that glorious pine needle juice into tannen honig, or pine honey.

Tannen honig is very hard to find in stores in the United States. First, as you may have heard, bees all over the world are dying from pesticides and mysterious diseases. Second, tannen honig can be harvested only in July and August. I haven't found any American pine honey. If you find any, let me know. And cats don't like honey, I think; I am not sure. But I had a dog once who did.

Tannen Honig

CHEESE

is best.
Especially hard cheese
like cheddar or Parmesan.
You can grate it.
You can slice it.
You can melt it.
You can grill or bake it
until it goes golden and crisp.
Best of all, you can eat it as it is,
in small sweet crumbly pieces.
Imagine a whole house
made of CHEESE.
Mmmm. Delicious.

Benji Davies

CAKE

Isabelle Arsenault

I never met a cake I didn't like.
But chocolate cake with
chocolate icing is my favorite!

Ramen
Dan Santat

Ramen is a Japanese dish that consists of Chinese-style wheat noodles served in a meat- or fish-based broth, often flavored with soy sauce or miso, and uses toppings such as sliced pork, dried seaweed, menma, and green onions. Nearly every region in Japan has its own variation of the dish.

ラーメン

Salad!

Greg Pizzoli

I like the arugula, I like the peas,
I like the tomatoes, and if you please,
I like avocado and I like corn,
I like to add sunflower seeds,
I like a garbanzo, a lentil, any kind of bean,
I like broccoli, and I like celery,
I like the carrots, the cukes, and currants,
but what I like most of all
is that nothing in my bowl
had parents.

Strawberry Daifuku

Misa Saburi

いちご大福

Mochi stuffed with
sweet azuki paste
and a fresh strawberry
is quite magical!

Berries

Brigette Barrager

My favorite food
is berries. They are
wild and sweet and
taste like summer!

FRENCH FRIES

LAURIE KELLER

SALT CLOUD

DO YOU know HOW French Fries are made? Well, the SUN is a GIANT POTATO and when its potato rays turn golden and CRISPY THEY fall to Earth! (The first one Landed in France, Which is WHY they're called French FRIES.)* Yum! They're SO DELICIOUS!

* This may not be the way they're made, but it sure tastes like it!

PRAWN

SQUID

LEMON

MUSSEL

PAPRIKA

OLIVE
OIL

SAFFRON

Chicken Alfredo

Shannon Wright

Whenever my dad made chicken Alfredo, it felt like
he had presented us with the grandest treasure.
Even now, all I see are sparkles when it catches my eye.

MATTHEW CORDELL

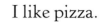

I like pizza.

I like pizza with veggies,
I like pizza with cheese,
I like pizza with extra cheese,
I like pizza with turkey pepperoni,
I like pizza.

I like deep-dish pizza,
I like thin-crust pizza,
I like medium pan-style crust pizza,
I like stuffed-crust pizza,
I like pizza.

I like homemade pizza with homemade crust,
I like homemade pizza with French bread crust,
I like frozen pizza,
I like delivery pizza,
I like restaurant pizza,
I like pizza.

I like pizza with a little bit of sauce,
I like pizza with the regular amount of sauce,
I like pizza with extra sauce,
I like pizza.

I like hot pizza,
I like warm pizza,
I like cold pizza,
I like pizza.

I like pizza.
I like pizza.
I like pizza.

Juliet Menéndez
Pitaya
FRUIT

Pitaya fruit, subtle and sweet, is my favorite food. As a little girl, I couldn't wait for the rainy season in Guatemala, when the pitayas would pop up along the cactus vines of Lake Atitlan and I could go with my cousins to pick them. We would climb along the rocks, hunting for them like treasures. Then we'd cut them into two little bowls and eat them right up with a spoon and a sprinkle of lime!

Matzo Ball Soup

Karen Katz

Every Passover I get to eat my
favorite food: matzo ball soup.
The matzo balls are light and fluffy.

Yum!

Ice Cream

Aki

*I*n autumn, winter, spring, or summer,
ice cream is always a good idea.

THE ERIC CARLE MUSEUM OF PICTURE BOOK ART

was created by Eric and Barbara Carle in 2002 to champion the importance of illustrated children's literature. The Carle, as it's known, collects and exhibits original drawings from artists around the world, showcasing a vibrant and innovative art form that inspires generation after generation of young readers. In addition to preserving a major collection of original art from the last century, the museum houses galleries, an art studio, picture book and scholarly libraries, and a theater, and offers educational programs for families, schoolchildren, educators, and scholars. The Carle is a place for visitors to get lost in a book, to talk about an exhibition, to make art, or to meet a favorite illustrator. It's a place for anyone who loves illustrated literature to learn about other cultures, share ideas, and get creative.

You can learn more about The Carle, including membership and how to plan for a visit, at carlemuseum.org.

Eric Carle is the author and illustrator of more than eighty books, including *The Very Hungry Caterpillar* and *Brown Bear, Brown Bear, What Do You See?* written by Bill Martin Jr. Eric was born in the United States but spent his early years in Stuttgart, Germany, where he studied art and design at the Academy of Applied Art. [eric-carle.com]

Benji Davies is the author and illustrator of *The Storm Whale* and the illustrator of *Big Friends* by Linda Sarah and *Goodnight Already!* by Jory John. As a child, Benji was often found painting at the kitchen table . . . a habit he has continued into adulthood. He lives in London with his wife, Nina. [benjidavies.com]

Author and illustrator **Isabelle Arsenault** studied graphic design at the Université du Québec in Montreal. Her work has appeared in several magazines in Canada and the United States. Her children's books have won many awards and distinctions, including three Governor General's Awards for Children's Literature and two *New York Times* Best Illustrated Books of the Year selections. Isabelle's style is infused with sensitivity and finesse that appeals equally to both children and adults. [isabellearsenault.com]

Dan Santat is the Caldecott Medal–winning and *New York Times*–bestselling author and illustrator of *The Adventures of Beekle: The Unimaginary Friend*, *Are We There Yet?*, and *After the Fall (How Humpty Dumpty Got Back Up Again)*. His artwork is also featured in numerous picture books, chapter books, and middle-grade novels, including Dav Pilkey's Ricky Ricotta's Mighty Robot series. Dan lives in Southern California with his wife, two kids, and many, many pets. [dantat.com]

Greg Pizzoli is an author, an illustrator, and a screen printer. His best-loved books for children include *The Watermelon Seed*, *Tricky Vic*, and *Good Night Owl*, among others. Greg's work has been featured in *The New York Times*, and he's won two Portfolio Honor Awards from the Society of Children's Book Writers and Illustrators. He lives in Philadelphia with his wife, artist Kay Healy; their dog; and two cats. [gregpizzoli.com]

Misa Saburi was born in Sleepy Hollow, New York; raised in Tokyo, Japan; and now lives in Brooklyn, New York. She is the illustrator of *Bearnard's Book*, written by Deborah Underwood, and *Monster Trucks*, written by Joy Keller. [misasaburi.com]

Brigette Barrager is an artist, a character designer, an illustrator, and a writer of children's books. The illustrator of the bestselling picture book *Uni the Unicorn* by Amy Krouse Rosenthal, Brigette earned a degree in character animation from the California Institute of the Arts, where she now teaches. Brigette lives and works in Los Angeles with her husband, Sean; a grumpy little dog; and two rascally gray kitties. [brigetteb.com]

Laurie Keller is the bestselling author-illustrator of many books for kids, including *Arnie the Doughnut*, *Do Unto Otters*, *The Scrambled States of America*, *Open Wide: Tooth School Inside*, and the Adventures of Arnie the Doughnut chapter book series. She lives on the shores of Lake Michigan. [lauriekeller.com]

Felicita Sala grew up in Australia, where she studied philosophy, then moved to Rome and became an illustrator. She has created several picture books, including *Joan Procter, Dragon Doctor*; *Mr. Crum's Potato Predicament*; and *Ode to an Onion: Pablo Neruda & His Muse*. She spends a lot of time sharpening pencils, cooking, and reading books to her daughter, Nina. [felicitasala.com]

Shannon Wright is an illustrator and a cartoonist based in Richmond, Virginia. She has illustrated a number of books, including *My Mommy Medicine* by Edwidge Danticat, *TWINS* by Varian Johnson, and *I'm Gonna Push Through* by Jasmyn Wright. During the summer she teaches a comics course at her alma mater, Virginia Commonwealth University. [shannon-wright.com]

Matthew Cordell is the author and illustrator of many books for children, including *Trouble Gum*, *Another Brother*, *hello! hello!*, and *Wish*. His book *Wolf in the Snow* was the recipient of the 2018 Caldecott Medal. He has illustrated the books of such renowned authors as Philip C. Stead (*Special Delivery*), Rachel Vail (the Justin Case series), and Gail Carson Levine (*Forgive Me, I Meant to Do It*). Matthew lives in suburban Chicago with his wife, the novelist Julie Halpern; and their two children. [matthewcordell.com]

Juliet Menéndez is an illustrator, a designer, and a teacher who divides her time among Antigua, Guatemala; New York; and Paris. Her current living arrangement reflects her roundabout education—a liberal arts school in Minnesota, an art school in Italy, French lessons at the Alliance Française in Guatemala, a design school in Paris, and a graduate program for bilingual education in New York. [julietmenendez.com]

Quilts, costumes, prints, sculpture, paintings, collage, book illustrations—**Karen Katz** has always been making something. Her love of folk art and children's art has influenced all her illustrations. She is the acclaimed author-illustrator of more than sixty-five books, including *Can You Say Peace?*, *Over the Moon*, *Counting Kisses*, and *Where Is Baby's Belly Button?* Karen and her husband live in New York City and Woodstock, New York, where you can usually find her gluing, painting, collaging, and having a good time. [karenkatz.com]

Aki, whose real name is Delphine Mach, is the author and illustrator of *The Weather Girls* and *The Nature Girls*. When she is not illustrating, Aki maintains a culinary blog, *The 3 Sisters*, that she shares with her sisters, who are equally passionate about cooking. [delphinemach.com]